the LIBRARY BOOK

by **Tom Chapin** and **Michael Mark**

illustrated by **Chuck Groenink**

SCHOLASTIC INC.

ISBN 978-1-338-28438-6

12 11 10 9 8 7 6 5 4 3 2 1   18 19 20 21 22 23

Printed in the U.S.A.   08

First Scholastic printing, January 2018

Cover design by Ann Bobco and Vikki Sheatsley; interior design by Ann Bobco
The text for this book was set in Base Nine.
The illustrations for this book were rendered digitally and in pencil.

The song "Library Song" is from the Tom Chapin album *Moonboat*.

For Willa, Elspeth, Myra Jean, Max, and Miles
—*Papa Tom Chapin*

To Mary Mark,
the greatest reading teacher in the known universe
—*Michael Mark*

For Mum, and Dad, for always keeping books on the shelves
—*Chuck Groenink*

Saturday morning
and the rain is pouring.

Dad worked late last night,

he's in there snoring.

Same old stuff on TV—boring.

So what if I can't go out and **play**;

I know what I'll do today.

I'm going down to the library,

picking out a book, check it in, check it out.

Gonna say **hi** to the dictionary, picking out a book, check it in, check it out.

Now **I** like books and **they** like me, so when I go to the library,

I sit down in my **favorite chair** and check to see **who's there.**

Maybe **one** book, maybe **two**.

"Take me home,"

says
**Winnie
the Pooh.**
"And
if we have
to travel
far,
I'll bring
my
honey
jar."

Oh, I'm going down to the library, picking out a book, check it in, check it out.

Gonna say hi to the dictionary,
picking out a book, check it in, check it out.

Sleeping Beauty **yawned** and **said,**

"I'll come when **I** get **out of bed.**"

But Madeline
says,
"Let her nap!"
and jumps
into
my lap.

The Cat in the Hat says, "Hey, I'll go."

"Don't take him!"
cries Pinocchio.
"Don't take that cat
to your address;
he always makes
a mess."

Oh, I'm going down to the library, picking out a book, check it in, check it out.

Gonna say **hi** to the dictionary, picking out a book, check it in, check it out.

Mrs. Parker's
back behind the checkout desk today.
The Cheshire Cat jumps on her head
and says,

"Let's play!"

But Mrs. P. says,
"Goodness,
are you sure
you want all these?"

"oh yes!"

we shout together.

She says . . .

"Shhh! Quiet, please!"

I'm going down to the library, picking out a book, check it in, check it out.

Gonna say **hi** to the dictionary, picking out a book, check it in, check it out.

The Seven Dwarfs begin to shout,
"Say,
take us with you.

**Check
us
out!**"

Then Cinderella
gets her
gown
and
Babar
grabs his
crown.

Then Curious George swings from the shelf.

Along comes Mother Goose herself.

Out the door we danced and sang.

The whole library rang.

Oh, I'm going down to the library, picking out a book, check it in, check it out.

Gonna say **hi** to the dictionary, picking out a book, check it in, check it out.

I'm going down to the li—

Shhh!

Picking out a book, check it in, check it out!